Dear Parent:
Your child's love of reading starts here!

Every child learns to read in a different way and at his or her own speed. Some go back and forth between reading levels and read favorite books again and again. Others read through each level in order. You can help your young reader improve and become more confident by encouraging his or her own interests and abilities. From books your child reads with you to the first books he or she reads alone, there are I Can Read Books for every stage of reading:

SHARED READING
Basic language, word repetition, and whimsical illustrations, ideal for sharing with your emergent reader

BEGINNING READING
Short sentences, familiar words, and simple concepts for children eager to read on their own

READING WITH HELP
Engaging stories, longer sentences, and language play for developing readers

READING ALONE
Complex plots, challenging vocabulary, and high-interest topics for the independent reader

ADVANCED READING
Short paragraphs, chapters, and exciting themes for the perfect bridge to chapter books

I Can Read Books have introduced children to the joy of reading since 1957. Featuring award-winning authors and illustrators and a fabulous cast of beloved characters, I Can Read Books set the standard for beginning readers.

A lifetime of discovery begins with the magical words **"I Can Read!"**

Visit www.icanread.com for information
on enriching your child's reading experience.

Show-and-Tell, Flat Stanley!
Text copyright © 2014 by the Trust u/w/o Richard C. Brown a/k/a Jeff Brown f/b/o Duncan Brown. Illustrations by Macky Pamintuan, copyright © 2014 by HarperCollins Publishers. All rights reserved. Manufactured in China. No part of this book may be used or reproduced in any manner whatsoever without written permission except in the case of brief quotations embodied in critical articles and reviews. For information address HarperCollins Children's Books, a division of HarperCollins Publishers, 10 East 53rd Street, New York, NY 10022.
www.icanread.com
Library of Congress catalog card number: 2013956397
ISBN 978-0-06-218976-9 (trade bdg.)— ISBN 978-0-06-218975-2 (pbk.)
Typography by Sean Boggs

13 14 15 16 17   SCP   10 9 8 7 6 5 4 3 2 1   ❖   First Edition

FLAT STANLEY

Show-and-Tell, Flat Stanley!

created by Jeff Brown
by Lori Haskins Houran
pictures by Macky Pamintuan

HARPER
An Imprint of HarperCollinsPublishers

Stanley Lambchop lived

with his mother,

his father,

and his little brother, Arthur.

Stanley was four feet tall,

about a foot wide,

and half an inch thick.

He had been flat ever since

a bulletin board fell on him.

Stanley's family was used to
him being flat.
They didn't think much about it,
except when Mrs. Lambchop
needed to clean behind the fridge.

Or when Mr. Lambchop
forgot his house key
(which happened quite a bit).
To the Lambchops,
Stanley was perfectly normal.

That's why Stanley was surprised

when Arthur asked,

"Can I take you to Show-and-Tell?"

Stanley frowned.

"You mean, because I'm—"

"So good at wiggling your ears!"

said Arthur.

"Miss Plum really wants to see it."

"Oh!" said Stanley.

"Sure, if Miss Plum said so . . ."

Stanley felt his face turning pink.

It always turned pink

when Miss Plum's name came up.

Miss Plum was the prettiest teacher

in the whole school.

"Thanks, Stanley!" said Arthur.

"No problem," said Stanley.

"That's what brothers are for."

Arthur smiled to himself.
He knew the real reason
Stanley was going to Show-and-Tell,
but he didn't say a word.

At school, Arthur's classmates

took turns showing and telling.

Sophie showed her mouse, Squeakers.

"He just loves cheese!" she said.

Manny held up

his grandpa's false teeth.

"My grandpa loves cheese, too."

Arthur introduced Stanley,

who wiggled his ears like crazy.

"My goodness!" said Miss Plum.

13

"Today I have something
for Show-and-Tell, too,"
Miss Plum added shyly.
She held out her left hand.
A big ring sparkled on her finger.

"I'm getting married!" said Miss Plum.

Stanley felt his heart sink.

Miss Plum? Married?

The other kids jumped up

and crowded around

to look at Miss Plum's ring.

"Let me see!" said Sophie.

She bumped into Manny.

Squeakers slipped out of her hands.

"Ouch!" said Manny. "Watch it!"

He dropped his grandpa's teeth.

The false teeth bounced twice,

then clamped onto Squeakers's tail!

"Wheeek!" squeaked Squeakers.

He took off running.

"Oh, dear!" cried Miss Plum.

She reached out to grab Squeakers,

and her new ring flew off her finger!

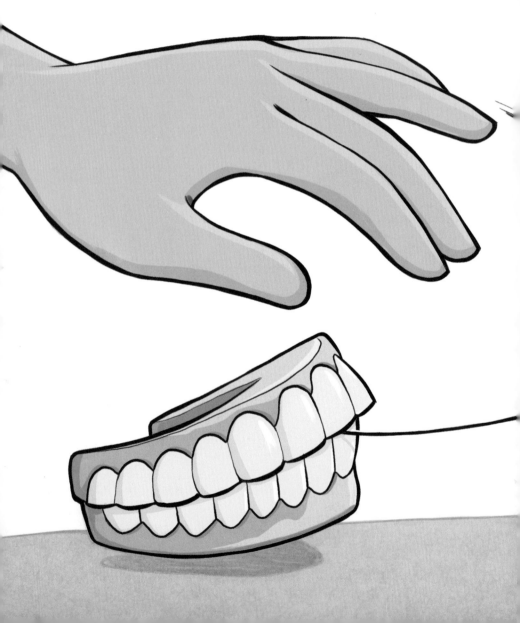

To Stanley, the ring seemed

to move in slow motion.

He watched it sail toward Squeakers—

and fall straight down

over the mouse's head,

where it landed like a sparkly collar

around his neck.

Poor Squeakers squeaked again

and ran even faster.

He zipped across the classroom,

scampered up a bookcase,

and vanished through a crack

in the ceiling tile.

"My mouse!" cried Sophie.

"My grandpa's teeth!" cried Manny.

"MY RING!" cried Miss Plum.

Stanley stood up.

"I'll save you, Miss Plum!

I—I mean, I'll save your ring.

And Squeakers. And the teeth!"

Stanley raced to the spot
where Squeakers had vanished.
"Arthur," he said.
"That crack in the ceiling—
it's like our window at home.
Give me a boost!"

"On the count of three!" said Arthur.

"One. Two. THREE!"

With a grunt, Arthur pushed Stanley

high over his head,

just as he had a dozen times before.

(Mr. Lambchop really did

forget his keys a lot.)

Stanley slid through the crack!

"I see Squeakers!" Stanley yelled.

"Come here, boy! Come on!"

Below, the students heard
crashing and thrashing as Stanley
chased the mouse over their heads.
"Go, Stanley, go!" yelled Manny.
"It's—no—use," Stanley said, panting.
"He's—too—fast!"

Then Arthur thought of something.

"Sophie, where's Squeakers's cheese?"

"Right here!" she said.

Arthur grabbed a slice

and flung it through the crack.

"Stanley, try this!"

The crashing stopped.

The thrashing stopped.

Then the class saw Stanley's arm

poke through the ceiling crack.

Squeakers sat in his hand,

happily nibbling the cheese.

Stanley's other arm poked out.

The false teeth and the ring

dangled from his fingers.

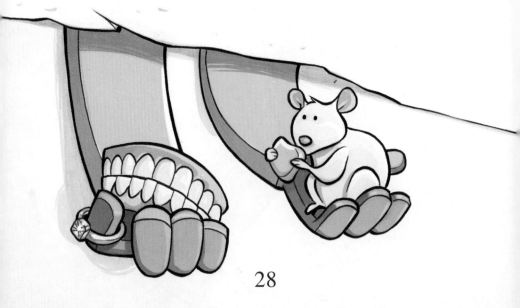

Last of all came Stanley himself,

stretching out of the crack

like a boy-sized strip of taffy.

"Oh, Stanley!" said Miss Plum,
once he was safely on the ground.
"You're my hero!"
She gave Stanley a big hug.
Stanley felt his face turn pink.
Bright pink.

"What's wrong with Stanley?"

asked Sophie.

Arthur grinned.

"His face always turns pink when—"

Then Arthur stopped.

He looked at Stanley.

"When he's been wiggling his ears,"

he said.

"Thanks, Arthur," whispered Stanley.

"No problem," said Arthur.

"That's what brothers are for!"